W9-BGX-770

I CAN'T GET
MY TURTLE
TO MOVE

I CAN'T GET MY TURTLE TO MOVE

Elizabeth Lee O'Donnell
Pictures by Maxie Chambliss

Morrow Junior Books
New York

Library of Congress Cataloging-in-Publication Data
O'Donnell, Elizabeth Lee.
I can't get my turtle to move / by Elizabeth Lee O'Donnell :
pictures by Maxie Chambliss.
    p.   cm.
Summary: A lively group of animals demonstrates numbers one
through ten—except for one lazy turtle that just won't move.
ISBN 0-688-07323-9.   ISBN 0-688-07324-7 (lib. bdg.)
[1. Animals—Fiction.   2. Counting.]   I. Chambliss, Maxie, ill.
II. Title.
PZ7.O2386Ic 1989
[E]—dc19   88-22046   CIP   AC

For Marta

One turtle sleeping in the sun.

"Walk!" I say.

"Blink," I say.

"Please?" I say.

But I can't get my turtle to move.

Two goldfish hiding in the weeds.
"Swim," I say, and they do.

But I can't get my turtle to move.

Three kittens tangling up the yarn.
"Purr," I say, and they do.

But I can't get my turtle to move.

Four puppies napping in the barn.
"Sit," I say, and they do.

But I can't get my turtle to move.

Five butterflies threading in and out.
"Sip," I say, and they do.

But I can't get my turtle to move.

Six inchworms hiking up a leaf.
"Munch," I say, and they do.

But I can't get my turtle to move.

Seven ants talking nose to nose.
"March," I say, and they do.

But I can't get my turtle to move.

Eight hens clucking on the fence.
"Peck," I say, and they do.

But I can't get my turtle to move.

Nine crows eating up the corn.
"Shoo," I say, and they do.

But I can't get my turtle to move.

Ten rabbits nibbling lettuce leaves.
"Hop," I say, and they do.

But I can't get my turtle to move.

One turtle sleeping in the sun.
"Hey!" I say. "Guess what?" I say. "Lunch!" I say.

I get my turtle to move!